Trapped in The Game 3

Tamicka Higgins

Disclaimer

This is a work of fiction. Names, places, characters and events are all fictitious for the reader's pleasure. Any similarities to real people, places, events, living or dead are all coincidental.

This book contains sexually explicit content that is intended for ADULTS ONLY (+18).

Where Were We?

"Anthony! Anthony, what the hell are you doing?"

"Give me a minute, Grant!"

I wasn't sure if I was going to make it out alive. I'd been in life or death situations before and each time I ended up on top. This was different though. This was the first time where I truly felt that I had something to lose. As a matter of fact, I had everything to lose.

It may have been a change in my mentality. Maybe, it was a part of what came with seeking happiness. The downside of having people in your life that you can't bear to part with. The devil always seems to show his face just when you think you've escaped hell. All I wanted was to get back home to see them again.

I'd had a family before, but it was never anything that I'd put above my aspirations. My former girl, she was okay. Her and I used to have late night chats about how much deeper I could go. She would push me to be the kingpin that I thought I wanted to be. In the hood that kind of ambition can lead you to be the boss. In reality, being the boss is an easy way to get a bounty put on your head.

I missed her at times whenever I managed to get a moment to reminisce. She used to champion my bullshit. Every gangsta appreciates a cheerleader. But that was all before I had Layla. She changed my destiny. I didn't want the power or respect anymore. I just wanted to be a real man, with a real family, and something worth going home to. I never expected that the *life* would work so hard to keep me in it.

I guess that you could say it was some odd karmic retribution that getting out was as difficult as it became. I loved my son. You could even say that I'd loved my former girl. Despite that, my past life wasn't one to envy. We were soldiers of fortune, who feared death—yet we taunted it at every turn. I was paying for every sin of my past, for every broken promise and deadly encounter—I had to pay for it all.

The problem was that it wasn't *me* anymore. I wasn't the killer or the Black Fate. I was just a man looking for his piece of peace. Even then, as I kept getting dragged deeper into the deadly fold, all I wanted was freedom from it.

Pastor Grant liked to preach about reform, and changing your insides enough that they would have a positive effect on your life beyond you. I used to think that was bullshit. Not anymore. Not then, when I had been so close to my dream of freedom and faced the constant threat of having it ripped away from me.

Layla wasn't too happy with me about the situation either. I left her in the dark as much as I could. I still had to call her, just to say goodbye. I wouldn't want to be one of those people who leave behind a path of regret when they die. At the very least, she didn't deserve to mourn me without some form of closure. I had to let her know that I tried.

***

She told me that she was pregnant. I proposed right after that and she accepted. I knew that she would still have some legal shit to work out with Vic, but I didn't care. I just needed her to know what was in my soul. Call it emotional if you want. You'd be surprised about the things that become important when you're facing death.

"Are you seriously making phone calls right now?"

I'd almost forgotten about Grant. I didn't answer him right away. I was pretty sure that he didn't know what was coming. Far be it from me to be the one to ruin his day before the bullets started to fly.

I stood in front of the cross and said a prayer. I didn't pray for myself—as one would expect from a man in my predicament. Instead I prayed for my dead son; I prayed for Darius—who was like a son to me—and I prayed that Layla would forgive me, whether or not I made it out of there on two feet or in a body bag.

"Alright, Anthony that's enough of the Verizon commercial. You said that you had some intel for me. Let's have it!"

As Grant came closer to me, the darkened church was illuminated by the reflection of red lights beaming off of the stained glass windows. It was the backup that he promised he wouldn't bring. Oddly enough, he looked just as shocked as I was to see them.

"I thought that this was just me and you Grant?"

"Oh, come on Black. What do you think I am, some kind of fool? Why the hell would I walk into a situation like this one without bringing some support?"

"You know what's funny…" The blistering sounds of motorcycle engines and souped-up muscle cars consumed the insides of the church. "I was thinking the same thing."

I dropped to the ground as bullets rained through the windows of the church. Grant screamed out, "What the fuck!" as the officers that he'd brought with him returned fire. He had no idea what had been going on. I took the opportunity to load and cock a gun of my own. Though I doubted that anyone else would barge into the church, I had to be sure that I was ready for them.

"Anthony, I swear to Christ, if you set this shit up!"

I had no time to answer. I knew that lectern in the church was bulletproof. Pastor Joy wasn't necessarily afraid of anyone trying to kill him, but he was in the room when Malcolm X was assassinated. He was a peaceful man, but he didn't expect that standard of decency to carry over to anyone else. Even men of the bible have to watch their backs—especially in that neighborhood.

I crawled up behind it, as the showers of gunfire continued in quick succession. Grant hid himself under the pews and tried to call up his guys to greenlight them to "fire at will" and "shoot to kill". It's interesting that he would think that either of us would have any control over the situation once it began.

"Anthony, you'd better put a stop to this shit right now!"

"And how the hell do you expect me to do that? With my magic nigga powers?!"

He screamed something inaudible and, in a blind rage, stood up and began to shoot at me from the other side of the lectern. I felt the impact of the gunfire from the other side, and heard the tile break. It shattered all around me, and fell in various-sized sharp pieces across the church carpet. I barely noticed that some of them had been covered in blood.

I thought that I may have been hit for a second. After a quick inspection of myself, I was certain that the lectern was in fact bulletproof; but I wasn't. I had to react quickly if I wanted to ensure that I wasn't taken out before I had a chance to escape.
I put my hand around the side and shot blindly in Grant's direction. I wasn't trying to hit Grant, it's just always a good idea to let the enemy know that you're packin' too. It tends to keep their bullshit to a minimum. He returned as much fire as he could and yelled out his threats. They didn't worry me too much.

As I reloaded, I assessed my chances of making it out of the church unscathed. As I did, a smoke bomb was thrown inside. After it went off, officers pounded on several of the doors trying to get it. At least, that's who I thought it was. At that point everything had fallen into such a state of chaos that everyone may have just been shooting at everyone else.

I took advantage of the smoke and used the spare seconds to push a pew against the side door closest to me and ducked back behind the lectern. I listened intently for Grant's coughing to make sure that he maintained his position out of my line of fire. I didn't want to kill him, but I was ready too.

Thinking that this may finally be it for me, I called Buzzy to let him know what to do in case I died. After I lost my son, I was ready to snap on the very next person to try me. Figuring that I would have to escape not long after that, I took up all of the cash that I had and stuffed it in the walls.

Buzzy helped to plaster everything back together. When shit went down, we just left it there. It seemed like a good backup plan, but I didn't have long to speak to Buzzy. I think that gunfire in the background may have spooked him a bit.

Whether or not he was high, he was naturally paranoid. It'd work out in my favor in case I died. He would assume that the worst had happened and act accordingly as soon as he got a chance to. I told him that, should the worst happen, to get the money and make sure that Layla and Darius were safe.

I knew that Layla had some family down south, as did Buzzy. I never bothered to make the connection before, but suddenly it seemed like that would be the move to make. It didn't help to worry about it then, but the information might have come in handy later on.

The officers outside didn't take too kindly to the stray bullets flying in their direction. One of them had balls enough to run up to the window and try to throw another smoke grenade in the church. He managed to get the door open, but paid for his brashness shortly after that with a stray bullet to the back of his head. Sad for him, but opportunity for me.

I pulled my shirt up over my face and tried to make a run for it through the side door. I figured that, with all commotion going on, no one would notice me slip by, especially since the outside now had a blanket of smoke blocking the visuals as well.

I was only a few feet from the door and near freedom. Before I could reach it, Grant jumped up from the pew and tackled me right beside Pastor Joy's private room. It took everything I had not to just shoot the prick—but, remembering that we were in church, I knew that was a line not to cross if it could be avoided. Jesus would forgive me but, if I got caught killing an officer of the law in God's house, the jury wouldn't. I thought to myself—*only do it if you have to.*

He got on top of me, put the gun to my head, and told me to stay still or he would pull the trigger. When I froze, he pulled a pair of cuffs from his side and began spouting off the Miranda rights to me as if we weren't in the middle of a fucking war. I thought that I was done. The police would kill all of Carlos's men, and I would be stuck to deal with the aftermath of what was sure to be dubbed the *church massacre* or some *hokey* shit like that.

Luckily for me, the Lord works in mysterious ways. In this particular situation, he worked in the form of Pastor Joy, hearing us scuffle right by his door. The pastor grabbed a weight from inside of his room and clobbered Grant over the head with it.

"Get up, young man. Hurry!"

"I thought that pastors were supposed to be peaceful?"

"Even the Lord had to know when restrained violence was the only solution. Is he okay?"

Grant was laid out on the floor, still and unresponsive. I checked his pulse—it seemed fine, but he was definitely going to be down and out for a good while. I helped Pastor Joy pull him into his room, and put Grant on the couch while the pastor covered up his head and tried to stop the bleeding.

"Thank you, Pastor."

"Don't thank me for this, young man. I'm not proud of it."

"Then why did you do it?"

"Look at him. He has been overcome by hubris and bloodlust. He shall learn his lesson in due time, but this is clearly not that day. Now quickly get in."

Pastor Joy led me to a bunker that led to the basement of the church. It spanned the length and width of the floor beneath the pews, but there was no escape route. The plan was for me to stay there until everything finally quieted down. It took longer than expected.

Leverage

For about an hour things seemed to get progressively worse. Carlos took my advice and invited every cholo in town to join in with the *festivities*. It was an all-out war on the streets between the cops and every criminal that you could imagine. I knew that the body count would be in the dozens, but the only way that I could make it back to my family was if a bunch of other people didn't make it back home to theirs. It's selfish, but I didn't ask for any of it.

I felt bad about it for a second. That was until I realized how peaceful the streets would be without all of these motherfuckers on them with their itchy trigger fingers, and yes that does include the assholes in blue uniforms. Call it justification, but someone had to pay for allowing the city to get this volatile. I was a product of the environment, not its creator...conscience cleared.

The firing continued until the swat team showed up to disperse the onlookers and *neutralize* whatever remained of Carlos's men. Unfortunately for me, that "they'll stay away from the church" theory that I had was only good for as long as the God-fearers were winning.

Soon after the swat team arrived, Carlos and his men ran into the church—ironically hoping to find some sort of sanctuary. I did my best to stay quiet—it was likely that they would shoot anything or anyone that didn't come into the church with them.

The floorboards were thick wood, but they weren't bulletproof, and I'm pretty sure that there's nothing in the Bible that says not to shoot the floor.

Regardless of the nerves dictating their impulse, I was pretty sure that a few of them were still salty about the drugs that Buzzy and I had sold them a few years back. I know that at least half of them would have loved to see my head on a pike in their front yard. Whether by accident or intentionally, I was still quite a long way away from being in the clear.

Pastor Joy left the safety of his room to greet the violent oncomers. He was black and they were Spanish. Historically, he should have been a dead man—but apparently being in God's employ acts as a "get out of murder free" pass. He tended to the wounded, but was sure to lock the doors behind him—as Grant would've likely been used as a bargaining chip if he were discovered there.

Carlos was with them but, for lack of better words, he looked like he had just been run through a fucking blender. They put him on one of the pews in the front of the church. He was bleeding so much that it started to seep through the wooden floors. It was a disgusting sight to see, but such is the truth behind the battles that we fight. Besides, I've got to hand it to him, he's a hard fuckin' guy to kill.

The firing stopped—at what seemed like all at once. Judging by the guys that had made it to the safe haven of the church, the cops had to have been pretty banged up themselves. I took a chance and left the safety of the basement to see if I could haggle myself a way out with the survivors that remained.

I went upstairs to Pastor Joy's room and waited for my opportunity to move. At that time I heard the gunshots continue, along with the sound of a big-rig barging down the narrow city street. The cholos in the church started to cheer, and flooded right back out the front door with their guns blazing.

When they filtered out, they left Carlos and the other incapacitated members in the church to fend for themselves, while Pastor Joy did all he could to help those with less severe injuries. I slowly crept out of the room and looked around to make sure that the coast was clear before I left.

I heard Grant grunting on the couch. I was nervous for a second—turns out that it was just pre-coma ramble. I was both happy that Pastor Joy hadn't killed him, and pissed the fuck off that he was still alive. I would have to deal with that problem later then—there was no time. That's not to say that the decision wasn't hard.

I left him there and exited Pastor Joy's room. I thought about leaving Carlos, but it didn't feel right. If he hadn't helped me to start that war, I would probably have been dead by then. At best, I would be handcuffed sitting in the back of a cop car, while in the middle of a different version of the same firefight. I picked him up and put his arm around my shoulder.

"What the hell are you doing?"

"I've got to get him help, Father."

"Would you look at him Anthony? He's already one foot in the grave. If you try to leave with him now, you'll both have a one-way ticket to the afterlife. What are you thinking?"

To be honest, I wasn't sure that I was thinking clearly. My ears were still ringing from my exchange with Grant and constant poundings from the streets outside. My vision had begun to phase in and out of clarity, but I didn't think much of it. I chocked it up to exhaustion.

"I owe this man my life. I can't just leave him here to die."

He looked at me with concern. I could tell that he wanted to ask me what I'd meant—but I'm pretty sure that he knew that the information would be of no use to him.

"Okay son. If you must go… take these."

He handed me his car keys.

"If you can make it around back, my car is parked in the garage furthest to the right. Continue down the back alley going west and you should be able to avoid all of this chaos."

"Thank you, Father."

We left through the side door of the church as officers threw yet another smoke bomb through the window. The last thing that I'd heard from Pastor Joy was a heartfelt, "Our Father" followed by shouting from a band of whoever the fuck won—I didn't care much who did.

***

Pastor Joy's car was an old hatchback, but it would have to do. Though I was worried that it wouldn't be fast enough, it turned out to be a gift in disguise—as no one seemed to suspect us as we barreled down the roads at eighty miles an hour.

Carlos was losing a lot of blood, and I wouldn't be able to just drop him off at the hospital without setting off a few red flags. Even if I had, there was no telling how lucid he would be, or whether or not he would snitch on me to the investigators that were sure to want to question him about what happened.

Against my better judgement, I took him to the motel where I had told Layla and Darius to stay—while I figured out that entire situation. In a selfish way, I still had just wanted to see her again. The primary thought in my mind was "fuck the circumstances".

It had to be way past midnight when we arrived at the parking lot.

Home

I had to toss my cellphone, so I couldn't be sure of what time it was and Pastor Joy's clock was notoriously wrong. In either case it was late enough that the streets were fairly empty and most of the city was quiet—so I didn't have to worry about too many peering eyes.

I pulled Carlos's limp body out of the backseat, and carried him to the room where Layla was staying. It was probably dumb, but I had to knock... really hard. I knew that she was probably sleeping and I didn't have time to be polite. I could barely keep a thought straight enough in my mind to form a sentence. All I could think of was trying to find the best place to bunker down while this all blew over.

"Tony. Oh my God! What the hell is going on?"

"I'll explain it to you later, Lay. But right now I need you to go grab your first aid kit and meet me in the room."

"Okay, it's in the car."

Layla ran to the car to get her first aid kit out of the trunk while I laid Carlos on the couch. I was only able to breath for a moment before she came back in and bombarded me with questions. It was the last thing that I needed at the moment. My heart was beating out of my chest and the world seemed like it was starting to spin.

“Tony, you need to tell me right now what the hell this is about!”

“Honestly, at this point—you might be able to see it on the news.”

“What!”

I turned on the television and searched the motel room for liquor to drink. We listened to the reports of what had been going on as she did her best to clean the blood off of Carlos’s body and find the wounds.

“Breaking News: Officers have surrounded a popular New City church and are currently at odds with an unnamed rogue informant. Reports declare that the suspect in question has holed up in the church and refuses to exit. We are told that all non-violent tactics to remove the suspect from the church have failed. Officers have released a statement mandating that all civilian vehicles are to remain clear of the roads in and around the nearby area, as they fear that the altercation may turn increasingly violent. All civilians are advised to remain indoors until such a time as this altercation is resolved. I’m Lauren Naples with Eyewitness News, and I will be right here with you covering this bizarre story as it unfolds.”

She covered her mouth in horror at the thought of what had almost become of me.

“Tony, what the hell did you do?”

“I did what I had to do to get out of the shit.”

"Are you hurt?"

"No. No just a few scratches. But, right now, I'm worried about this guy."

"Oh... Right." She began to address Carlos's wounds before it occurred to her to ask, "Who is he?"

"Him...?" I wanted to lie more than I'd wanted to breathe at this point. "That's Carlos." But I couldn't.

"Carlos! You want me to help 'Mr. cut Buzzy's hands off' Carlos?"

"It was only one hand and I know it sounds crazy, but listen."

"I'm not listening to shit."

She walked over to me and checked my head for cuts and bruises.

"What the hell are you doing, Lay?"

"I'm looking for where you bumped your head, because something is clearly wrong with you."

""Is this really a time for jokes?"

"I'm not joking." She pulled her hand from behind my head and it was covered in blood. "Tony, I need to take care of this right now."

"What about him?"

"Listen, I know that—for whatever reason—you want to help him, but I'm not taking care of him before I take care of you. Even if I wanted to, I don't have anything here that could help him. He's bleeding too much."

"What does he need?"

"He needs a hospital, Tony. If you really want to help him; that's the only way."

At that moment, I started feeling dizzy. I couldn't afford to pass out there. On the off chance that someone had followed me to the motel—we would've had to be out of there anyway.

I pulled out Carlos's phone, and dialed 911. When they asked what the emergency was, I told them that "a man has been shot" and gave them the address. They asked me to stay on the line to answer some questions but, for obvious reasons, I didn't do that. I left the phone next to Carlos's body and screamed for Layla to get her things and get in the car

I went into the bedroom and picked up Darius while Layla waited for us in the driver's seat. I put Darius in the car and asked her, "How did you pay for the room?"

"In cash, baby."

"Good. I love you."

I kissed her on the lips. She pulled out of the parking lot and drove west as fast as she could while an ambulance pulled into the motel parking lot. As my heart rate slowed, I started to feel the effects of the head wound. Layla had to keep slapping me to keep me awake.

Worry

We drove for about a half hour. At least that's how long I think we were on the road. By then, I'd already been drifting in and out of consciousness. I couldn't really see straight, but I was able to keep my head up for long enough increments of time to keep myself from blacking out completely.

I didn't notice how much I'd been bleeding but, from the look on Layla's face, I knew that it was bad enough to warrant some concern. I was worried, but not as much as I was about making sure that we all got to a safe place to collect ourselves and make a game plan. They usually come naturally to me, but I couldn't come up with anything. Thank God that I had Layla to hold on to the reins while I tried to piece everything together.

The roads seemed to blend in with the streetlights, and music all sounded like white noise. Whenever my eyes would drift closed for too long, Layla would jerk the car to throw me around and jolt me awake. A few times, I think that she just did it out of anger, but it worked all the same.

I wasn't sure where she was going and, in all honesty, I didn't care. I knew that we were heading west; that meant that we were getting farther away from the hell that we'd just escaped, and that was good enough for me.

She swore that she asked me a few times where we should go, and that I answered "*Le' Fitz.*" I don't remember the conversation, but I've since just taken her word for it. I don't like thinking about that day too much—it's never fun to face your mortality. I kept the conscious thought in my mind that, when the car finally came to a stop, I would force myself up with the little energy that I had. "Thoughts make the body work"—it was a leftover lesson from Buzzy's mother.

We got to a *Ritz*-like hotel not long after that. It sounds like a bad idea in theory, but classy hotels do well at keeping their guests—and the business of their guests—on the *hush-hush*, as long as you're willing to leave a generous tip. We valet-parked the car and entered the hotel. My bleeding head got a few stares but, once again, people tend to mind their own business in fancy places—especially that late at night.

I gave Layla a few hundred bucks to give to the guy at the main desk. It was a crap-shoot, but it was the only way that we'd be able to get a room anonymously. I figured a hundred would be enough for him to keep our presence in the hotel a secret, should anyone come looking for us.

While Layla checked in, Darius and I walked around the lobby of the hotel. Layla told him to make sure that I stayed awake while she checked us in. I think a part of her also wanted me to help explain to Darius exactly what was going on. In her defense, she had no idea either. They had the tendency of getting information from me in pieces.

"What happened, Tony?"

"Nothing crazy, I just hit my head."

There was a television hanging on the wall. The volume was off, but the crawl on the bottom of the screen told enough of the story that any idiot could decipher what had been going on. I'd hoped that Darius wouldn't notice it, but kids have a bad habit of finding the exact thing that you're trying to keep from them.

"Does it have to do with that?"

He pointed at the T.V. The reporters had been doing a good job with their shaky camera bullshit and exaggerated gasps every time they heard a fucking gunshot. I never thought that I'd look at some shit like that and know for sure that it was overplayed, but I guess that's the only way to get the public excited. That's not what he meant when he asked, but I couldn't help but acknowledge the inconsistency.

That said, I watched it with him and feigned awe—for his sake. I didn't want to tell him that it was me who started that whole thing. I was always afraid of giving him the wrong image to look up to. It might sound arrogant, but I had to take into account that he looked up to me.

I tried to keep it as general as possible. I wasn't really ashamed of what I'd done, but just didn't need him thinking that situations like that always work out in the end. Kids are too impressionable to allow certain kinds of nuance.

The fact of the matter was that I just didn't want him following in my footsteps; Layla was already scared to death of him idolizing my past life, or his father's current one. The best thing that I could think to do was tell the closest thing to the truth that I could, without glorifying it too much. A good parent always knows how to find the lesson.

"Sort of. But it's something that I would have avoided if I had a choice."

"Why didn't you have a choice?"

"Because I made too many of the wrong ones. Sometimes, there's a limit to how much life will let you fuck up before it starts to take away your options. Mine were cut down to two. If I did the other thing, I wouldn't be here right now. I wouldn't be anywhere, and you and your mother would be sad. I couldn't let that happen."

"Could you have stopped it?"

"I keep trying. It's not always that easy."

"Is that why you've been acting funny ever since we got back from vacation?"

"What do you mean? I've been around."

"Not really. Even when you are, you and Ma are always arguing."

He wasn't wrong. Honestly, I hadn't had a moment's rest since the funeral. Whether it was Grant's nonsense or Carlos's fucking shenanigans or even Buzzy's constant fuck-ups, something was always dragging me away from them.

"I'm just trying to clean up some of the dirt that I've left behind. It's nothing to worry about."

“She’s afraid that one day you won’t come home. I told her not to worry because I’m here to take care of her.”

“And I’m proud of you for that. But you shouldn’t be worrying about that kind of stuff at your age.”

“I know. It’s not that I’m worried, I just want her to be okay… She likes you a lot. I think more than my dad.”

“Also, not something that you should be thinking about.”

“Then what am I supposed to think about?”

My attention was caught by the reporters on the T.V. who were still covering the firefight at the church. I hate to say that I was ignoring the kid, but I couldn’t help but worry about whether or not Pastor Joy had gotten out of there alive. When I left he was still tending to the wounded, but that had been over an hour before then. If they were still shooting it might still have been in a tight spot.

I was worried about Grant to an extent too, but that was more so because a dead officer just means more attention that would be directed my way when that shit finally ended. I did my best not to stress it, but how couldn’t you?

My entire existence was out of my hands; there was a war in the middle of the city, and I had gotten a bunch of people killed for no damn reason. Yet, there I was checking into a five-star hotel like I’m a fucking Kardashian or some shit. Some people don’t see their punishment coming; I was anxiously awaiting the fucking shoe to drop.

Layla walked over to us smiling, with a full plastic bag and two key cards in her hand. Before she could get close enough to hear, I looked at Darius and told him something that most fathers don't get a chance to tell their sons.

"Worry about this moment. You see this second right now; where everything's okay?"

"Yea."

"Remember it. Never forget it. Never forget that how you feel right now is okay. Stay in the now and, if ever you find yourself lost... you fight your way back to it. Understood?"

"Yes, sir."

"Good. Now, go help your mother with the bags."

He went to go help his mother with our things as I finished watching the news report. I'm not sure what I was looking for—maybe something to ease my guilt. Whatever it was, I didn't find it there.

"Tony, come on!"

"I'm coming."

I got up as slowly as I could to keep my head from spinning. Layla wrapped her arm around mine and helped me to the elevator. We got a little attention from the worried staff, but it didn't matter. We were already in and the blood that I left on their window was already there. They never make you clean up after yourself in places like that.

We got into the elevator, and headed up to the twentieth floor. Layla managed to get us a decently-sized suite. I had to admit that I was impressed, but also a little worried at how she was able to get us such a nice spot on short notice.

"How'd you get a room this nice, so late?"

"You said to tip the guy well."

She smiled, as I realized that she'd tipped the guy behind the counter way more than I had recommended. I couldn't get mad as I kind of deserved it. It was a cute couple moment.

At least Darius thought that it was funny.

***

We rushed to the room. Layla made a point to put Darius down for bed as soon as we got in. He protested, but that came to an end once she gave him the *angry mom* look. I was surprised to see him comply so easily. When I'd first met him, he had a nasty disrespectful streak of behavior. I was glad to see him grow out of it a bit. He was becoming a good kid.

I put some coffee on and sat on the couch. Once Layla was done with Darius, she came into the living room with me—all of her medical supplies in hand—and asked me if I was ready for inspection. I got myself a cup of coffee and grabbed two sample bottles of vodka from the minibar. She watched me chug one, and then proceeded to chug the other.

She put her hands around my jawbone and kissed me on my forehead.

“I love you, you idiot.”

“Hey, is that necessary?”

“After the day you put me through Tony, you’re lucky I didn’t add a few more bruises to you.”

“You got a point.”

We laughed for a second. She turned the television on to cover up my grunts.

“Anything but the news please, Tony. It’s gonna make me sick.”

“Okay, baby.”

She grabbed a pair of tweezers and began to pull random debris from the back of my head. Apparently the lectern was bulletproof, but it didn’t help too much for the random debris and shrapnel that flew off it. A bunch of it had ended up lodged in my head. Luckily enough though, it didn’t hit anything vital. It still hurt like a bitch though.

“Stay still, Tony. I’m almost done.”

Every time she pulled her hand back to dump the shreds of metal and tile onto the coffee table, there was more blood. I was starting to get dizzy, but I did my best to not pass out from the blood loss. We’d probably end up having to pay for the blood stains that I left on the couch.

When she was done, she took a sewing kit and sewed up the major cuts that the pieces had left, and topped it all off with a stinging round of rubbing alcohol and a few Band-Aids. It was the most time that we'd spent alone together in weeks.

I sat back on the couch, my head was still pounding but I felt decent enough. She warned me not to go to sleep and poured me a cup of coffee. She fell asleep in my lap shortly after that—while we watched a movie. As soon as I was sure that she had fallen asleep, I turned the channel back to the news. She asked me not to, but I had to know how it all ended or, better yet, if it had at all.

"Carnage and pandemonium on the streets of New City, as the hostile war between police and a slew of what police are calling 'the who's who of gang affiliates' has finally come to a brutal conclusion. Several officers have been pronounced dead; others are in critical condition—and a countless number of their assailants have been captured or killed. There's no word yet on exactly what catalyzed this bloody conflict; but we have word from the chief of the New City Police Department that a thorough investigation will be done to find the cause. Stay tuned for more on this developing story."

There was still no mention of me. That had to be a good sign. Maybe not a great one, but I was willing to celebrate any minor victory. If Grant survived, there would more than likely be a team of New City's finest looking to get a piece of me. If and when they came looking, I'd have to go.

Only a fool would think that they could avoid them for much longer than I already had. The only question in my mind about it all was whether they'd arrest me or kill me while it was still easy to.

Escape was fast becoming a less likely option—by then, the city had to have been sealed off. We always try not to think about reality when it's that bleak, but those who work in ignorance tend to get dealt with one way or the other.

For the time being I was safe, and my fucking head was pounding. There was no sense in worrying about shit that I couldn't control—especially then. It's hard to be content sometimes but, just like I told Darius, I had to fight for my moment of peace.

Zeroes

We spent two days bunkered down in the hotel room. Layla and Darius took a few trips outside to feel like they were still a part of the civilian world. I pretty much just slept and tried to plan my next move.

I had to throw out all of our cell phones. It didn't seem like anyone was looking for me at the moment, but you could never be too careful. All it would take was one slip up and it would be game over.

I had Layla pick us up some cheap pre-paid phones from the corner store, so that we could keep in touch whenever they left the hotel. They each only had an hour or so worth of minutes on them; they were clunky, and the reception was shit—but it was something. I felt a little guilty at the sudden downgrade in our lifestyle, but I like to think that the two of them took it in stride.

It wasn't an ideal situation for any of us, but I was working on improving it. We still had some money left over from the heist. Layla had left the bulk of it at her apartment, hoping that it would be safe there when we returned. I thought it was crazy at first, but there's no better place to hide money that you can't deposit into a bank than in your woman's crib. She had no warrants, and as far as I knew there was no probable cause.

I could've gone there first to pick it up but, if the cops were any good at their jobs, that was the first place that they would go looking for me. They wouldn't be able to search for the money—then again, what use would we have for it if I was in jail?

The next idea was—of course—plan zero. I had left the house to Carlos and his goons, but I never told them what was in the walls. It may have been dumb of me not to dig into them and get it when I had the chance to but, as you should recall, I was kind of preoccupied with staying alive at the time.

The money was secondary back then. It also didn't help that Carlos was out of his fuckin' mind. All of that bullshit aside, there was a good chance that the money was all still right there beneath the sheet rock. I did the math in my head and figured that it might be just enough to get gone, and stay gone for good. Layla wouldn't be too happy about it—but money was running low. Even if she didn't like the idea, we wouldn't be able to stay locked in that hotel room forever.

"And what happens if you get caught?"

"I'm not going to get caught. I'll take the backroads back to the safe house and, when I get there, you can meet me here and we'll go."

"Go where, Tony? I'm not going to be bouncing around the world for the rest of my life. You have a family now! You can't just come and go when you please anymore. We need stability."

"That's what I'm trying to do, Lay. How do you expect to do anything without it? Or have you forgotten that we can only afford another night here before we're out on the street?"

"No, I haven't forgotten anything, but obviously you've forgotten that you're going to be a father! We can't live this way anymore!"

"Well, if you have another idea, my ears are open."

"We can just go, Tony. We can leave the state, put a down payment on a shitty little apartment and build up from there."

"And when that money runs out?"

"You get a normal fucking job and raise your child!"

"What the hell do I look like to you? Working some nine-to-five wearing a shirt with a fucking burger logo on it?"

"Oh I don't know… like a goddamn man! A responsible fucking adult! Like a fucking father! Pick one!"

"And that's really what you want. To get by paycheck to paycheck? Worrying about where our next meal is coming from?"

"I don't give a fuck about any of that, Tony! I just want to be normal again. Why is it so hard for you to accept that?"

"It's not…"

“Then why do you keep fighting it? Why do you keep running? You said you wanted a family. We’re right here. What else do you think you need to do, Tony?”

“I just want to provide you with the life that you deserve.”

“And you can do that, without being Black, or Negro, or Destino. Just be you.”

“I am being me.”

“No, you’re not. You’re being the *old* you.” She walked over to me and put my hands on her stomach. Our child was just beginning to grow. “This. This is bigger than the *old* you. This is your *new* life. That means a new you. That means *us*. I just want you to see that before you lose it.”

There are very few things as humbling as becoming a father. I’d gotten so wrapped up in *winning*, that I forgot what the fucking prize was. I hated when I had lapses in judgement like that. I’d like to blame it on the concussion that I’d gotten the night before but, if I’m being honest, I’d always been that way.

It was a problem that had long led me to make a bunch of self-destructive decisions. I had an obsession with winning; whether I summoned the battle or not. It was a problem that I couldn’t shake. It was pride, mixed with a lack of perspective. My impulses ruled me at the exact wrong moments.

Pastor Joy used to talk about pride in his sermons. I’m thinking that I should have paid more attention. That’s a hell of a fucking wake-up call from irony. The good thing was I’d been through it enough to know when I’m fucking up. That was one of those times. Layla was right. I'd gotten lost in myself yet again.

Despite that, no matter how right she was—the facts are the facts. We were running out of money. Even if I had decided in that moment to give it all up and get out of New City for good, we'd still have to face the reality of being penniless in the streets until the police did eventually get a hold of me. So we did what all good parents do. We compromised.

"Okay, how about this…? You go back to the apartment. If the cops are there, then you call me and just come straight back here. While you're doing that, I'll go to the safe house."

"What if someone's there?"

"You saw Carlos. He'll be down and out for at least a couple of weeks. Even still, they'll probably just throw him in jail the second that he's good enough to stand straight. His goons know better than to intrude when he's absent."

"You sure about that?"

"Sure enough to try."

"Baby…"

"Just, hear me out. If there's anyone there, I'll call you and meet you right back here. If we leave soon, we can be back here and on the road by tonight."

"Okay."

"Okay. You sure?"

"Yea. If we don't, what else are we gonna do? Just promise me that you'll be safe."

"I will. You too."

"I'm not the one that needs to be worried about... How's your head?"

"Good. Pounding. But, good."

"Come here."

We sat on the couch. I laid my head on her chest while she checked my stitches.

"I love you, you maniac."

"I love you too."

I like to think that I was honest with Layla about my ambitions for the future. Looking back, I may not have lied to her intentionally, but I was definitely lying to myself. I knew that there was no happy ending here. I knew that truth even before Buzzy and I had spoken about it. But, even with the threat of doom, I had to fight for something. I had to fight to keep this for as long as I could.

I didn't mind knowing that I may end up dead or in jail. What bothered me more than any of that was the thought of not ensuring that my family—and our unborn child—would be able to survive without me. Sacrifice is only your enemy when you don't embrace the idea that it's your duty. I'd risk it all for them that day, and I'd do it every day for eternity if I could.

We all have to die someday anyway. We could do worse than pretending that we did it on purpose.

Objetivo

We had the plan all settled. I got dressed and made sure that my gun was cleaned and loaded. My bad habit of overthinking and expecting shit to go wrong was still my closest ally. It made Layla a little uncomfortable, but I had to be sure that I was ready. They packed their bags and waited for me to send them off.

Layla and I had left around the same time. The two of them left the hotel a little before I did. I anticipated being caught somewhere along the line but, at the very least, I knew that they would be safe. I had Layla arrange a rental car for me to pick up about ten minutes after her and Darius were on the road. When it arrived, I got in, and headed toward the safe house.

I had to be careful to drive as normally as I could. It wouldn't normally be a concern—but my head was still pounding pretty badly. It took a lot not to swerve at times during the twenty-minute drive. Doctors say that, when you feel that way, it's best to pull over and take a break. For obvious reasons, that wasn't an option.

I got to the safe house at about six in the afternoon. It was the best time for any attempt at getting things done. Ever since the shootout at the church, most people were afraid of being out on the streets after dark. I texted Layla on her *burner* phone to make sure that she was okay. She answered quickly, and I smiled. I should have been more suspicious that everything had been going so perfectly. I'm too jaded to accept smooth goings-on.

I got out of the car and knocked on the door to the safe house. After my last encounter with Carlos there, I knew better than to barge in. I was about to break the handle off when someone answered.

"Hola, Negro. We've been expecting you."

The guy politely invited me in. I gripped the handle of my gun and walked in before him. Carlos and I had made a deal prior to the shootout that he wouldn't allow me to be killed once our business together was done. Locked up or not, his people tended to be compliant with whatever rules he'd set in place. Although, they didn't have much of a choice, if they wanted to keep their hands.

I was led into the living area where several of them had escaped to, while the police were busy rounding up the secondary members and cleaning up the corpse of their fallen brethren off of the ground. It was easy enough to figure out that they were supposed to meet Carlos there, after everything was said and done. It got me thinking that I should have just left his ass in the church. Then again, it counted as a favor—I figured that it might come in handy later on.

The first guy led me to the temporary *chicano* in charge. His name was Marcus. He was a scruffy looking guy, but more sensible than his appearance might suggest. He had a bit of a problem keeping eye-contact though. It caught me off guard; those guys are usually all about that *macho* shit. Then again, it could've just been a result of war with the cops and subsequent mourning.

He and I had indirectly met some years back. I'm not sure if he recognized me or not—we were both young men back then. In any case, he'd definitely known me for the shit that'd been going down for the previous few months.

It was my fault that his boss was teetering on death's doorstep at the moment. On the flip side of that, I was also the reason that he had his temporary position of power. Needless to say, I wasn't sure what to expect from our conversation.

"What the hell are you doing here, Negro?"

"I came to pick up a few things that I've left behind."

"Like what?"

"I'm not really at liberty to say. But it's something very important to me."

"If you're not at liberty to say, then I am not at liberty to assist you cabron."

It didn't really make sense to argue. I was out numbered and, as far as they knew, their leader was dead because of me. They would've jumped at the chance to let that shit get hostile. Then they'd just consider my death an act of retaliation. I remembered the conversation that I had with Layla and decided to just let it go. There was no thinking my way out of that problem. I just hoped that Layla had better luck than I would.

As I tried to make my out of the house, two of the guys stood in front of me and blocked my way into the hall. They didn't look ready to shoot, but apparently Marcus wasn't done talking to me.

"Sit back down, cabron. I wasn't finished."

"Alright. Is there something that I can do for you?"

"As of now… no. I'm not one to make deals with the likes of you. You are faithless, and with no tribe."

"Accurate."

"I do not trust such men."

"Then why are we talking?"

"Because, I fear that I may not have another opportunity to tell you. You're a marked man. Your lifespan is short. Carlos's protection will only last you for as long as he breathes. The moment that is no longer true, these men that you see—along with countless others that you do not—will rain down death on you for what you've caused. And it will be on my order."

"And why would you tell me that?"

"Every dead man deserves to know that it's coming. It gives you time to get your affairs in order. Besides, I'm curious what people do when they know that death is coming for them."

"Well, thanks for the heads up. Can I go now?"

"Sure Negro. Vamanos!"

"Good. Don't forget this conversation. It'll be fun to talk about later."

"Was that a threat?"

"Nope. Just accepting your invitation."

It was a classic gangsta exchange. I'm not sure what exactly made Marcus feel so confident about openly threatening me like that, but he knew better than to act in that moment. Even the most wild of cholos know that's it's bad for their health to go against direct orders.

It was an old school trick. The secret to overcoming the dull stares and sounds of hands reaching to their sides for their loaded weapons, is to stay fearless; at the very least, you have to convince them you are. I'd killed at least one person that everyone in that room knew personally. The trick with killing is that, once you get away with that many, people stop hating you and start fearing you.

I called Marcus's bluff and reached for my own gun. It was risky, but I had a good way of determining a motherfucker's stink eye and the bitch behind it.

"You've got some big cajones, cabron."

"Well, it's not like I didn't expect to die today. The question is, did you?"

He threw his hand in the air. "Get the fuck out of here."

The room fell silent as the men cleared the hall and watched me exit the safe house. I didn't have the money but, when I caught a glance into the room, the wall had still looked pretty much untouched, other than a framed picture.

I'd have to have Buzzy come for the money later on. I hoped that he still had a decent rapport with those assholes. His love of the Spanish world had really proven itself useful up to that point. Regardless of how much I may have just pissed them off, it stood to reason that Buzzy would still be a guest of honor to some extent. Either that or they would cut his other fucking hand off.

With that idea burned, I decided to rely on *plan B*. I called Layla when I got in the car. She didn't answer, but my exchange with Marcus hadn't lasted long; I figured that she may have still been driving. I thought of swinging by the house to meet up with her, but we had a plan and I promised to stick to it. I trusted her to call me when I got back to the hotel.

The drive back was difficult but I managed to get by without crashing the car. My headache was better, but I'd still been sporadically losing consciousness. I had to pull over a few times to wait out the dizziness and I figured that I was driving at about half-mile intervals, before the pain would return. With all that said, I made it back to the hotel in one piece, and got a valet to take care of parking the car.

The room was empty when I got back. I was still early, so I didn't stress it too much. My head had still been pounding pretty bad, so I made myself a drink and waited on the couch. I expected that Layla would be there soon. She wasn't one to deviate much from an agreement. I didn't even notice myself falling asleep.

They say that, on your deathbed, you can see the faces of your loved ones. It was a child's tale. Something that they used to tell kids so that they wouldn't have nightmares. That night, I was as close to death as I'd ever been—I dreamt of fire.

It's not that I feared hell, I feared the road that had led me there and I feared the times that I would be forced to return. I was never very big on doing the right thing until recently. Maybe that's why I never dreamt. I did that night though. As horrifying as the idea of staring the devil in the face can be, it was the best sleep that I'd gotten in a while.

"Tick, Tock"

I was woken up by a call on the hotel phone a few hours later. I was still dizzy and not sure how much time had passed.

"Hello?"

"Good evening, sir. I apologize for disturbing you at such a late hour. We've received a message for you and were told to hold it until nine o'clock tonight. We'd hoped to see you before then but, as the business day is coming to a close, it was imperative for me to ensure that you got the message before my shift ended for the day."

"What time is it now?"

"It's a little before ten, sir. I do apologize once again, but due to the circumstances..."

"It's fine. What's the message?"

"It reads: 'Tick Tock'. The caller in question left his name only as 'Grant'."

There were a million things that went through my mind at that moment. As you could imagine, none of them were good.

"Sir? Sir, are you still there?"

“Yes. Thank you very much.”

“It’s my pleasure, sir. And since I’ve got you, there is the matter of your check-out date. How long do you intend on continuing your stay?”

Layla and Darius had already packed their things. I didn’t have much with me other than the clothes on my back and the crap left over from Layla patching me up a few days before then. But Layla wasn’t back. Something was wrong.

“Extend it until tomorrow. I’ll update with you guys then.”

“Very good, sir.”

I searched the room up and down, careful not to make too much noise. Patrons of high-rate hotels like to bitch about whatever they can. When I finished searching the apartment, I looked at my burner phone. I had one missed call and no messages. I tried to call Layla on hers, but it went straight to voicemail.

My immediate fear was that she’d finally given up on me. It wouldn’t be too hard to understand if she had gotten free of my bullshit and decided to just take the money and run. I thought of our conversation earlier that day, and decided not to indulge too much in that worry.

There wasn’t much that I could do as long as her phone was off. Even if it wasn’t—if she was really trying to get away from me—she would’ve just trashed it altogether. I took a drink from the mini-bar and tried to decide what my next move should be.

If I just grabbed all my shit and ran, I could basically have had another shot at that whole “getting out of the game” fantasy that I’d been failing miserably at attaining. But if something went wrong, if she was in trouble, that meant that she’d needed me. I tried calling her a few dozen more times as I crept slowly toward a complete mental breakdown.

I intended to stay put, until someone or something reached out to tell me what to do. I had no idea where to go. If she ran, I’d never find her. If she was caught, it wouldn’t help anything if I was captured right alongside her. As I reached for another drink from the mini-bar, I got another call on the hotel phone. This time it was a different number.

“Hello?”

“Hello again, sir. This is the representative from the front desk.”

“What number is this?”

“I don’t think that’s of the utmost importance right now. I couldn’t tell you while I was inside, but there are some angry looking officers searching the building for you. Due to our confidentiality clause, I couldn’t tell them where your room was. But I’m almost certain that my manager may.”

“And where’s your manager?”

“Talking to them behind the desk. There isn’t much time. If you want to get out of there a free man, you’ll need to act quickly. There is an employee elevator at the end of the hall to the right of your location. Go to it, and dial the numbers *5-5-2-6-3-*

9. It will take you down to the employee parking lot. I'll meet you there with your car."

"And what the—?"

He hung up on me before I had a chance to ask him who the fuck he was, or how much he knew. I guess it didn't matter. When I looked out of my window, there were a fleet of police cars peppered throughout the parking lot. I had to move quickly.

I took the liter bottle of vodka and some painkillers with me. I'm not one for running drugs and liquor, but it seemed like it was going to be a busy night. If I was going to even attempt to get out of it alive and free, I'd have to do something to help me ignore that pounding fucking headache.

I ran down to the right end of the hall and dialed in the passcode. It took the elevator a while to get to me. By the time it did, you could hear the rushed footsteps of at least a dozen officers rallying up the hallway stairs. As the doors of the elevator opened and I got in, I heard the leader of the bunch shout out my room number and signal the men to get into position. I think they were ready to kill me.

I took the elevator straight down to the employee lot. When I saw that it was basically empty, I pulled out my gun and aimed. Whatever was going on, didn't seem like it was going to go away quietly. As I turned out of the elevator, my car pulled up behind me—with the front desk clerk from our check-in day, behind the wheel. He left the keys in the ignition and got out.

"Your vehicle, sir."

"Thanks. Let me ask you… why?"

"Because at this hotel, our guests are treated like family."

"Really? Is that it?"

"May I be candid, sir?"

"Sure."

"You're a badass and your wife tipped me a thousand dollars. This is the least that I could do."

"Okay… Thanks." I'd be lying if I said that I wasn't flattered.

He smiled and waved at me as I got in the car and sped off onto the street. I didn't know what the fuck he was talking about then. If I'm being honest, I still kind of wish I didn't know.

I didn't have a plan. I did my best to keep my focus and to keep things in perspective, but now my brain suddenly had another reason to beat against my skull. If she left me, I wasn't sure what I would've done. In a way, every decision that I'd made up to that point was for her. I just wanted to find a way for us to be together and to finally be happy.

It's almost impossible to push away the damning thoughts that consume you in moments of uncertainty. For me, it took everything that I had not to just drive to the nearest bridge and speed off the side of it. If I was alone, there was no reason to be alive anymore. I was done fighting. Luckily for me, saner heads prevailed, and being *sure* overtook the suicidal thoughts.

Granted

I tried calling Layla a few more times before I gave up on it altogether. The roads seemed to be filled with every cop in the country. I did my best to avoid the checkpoints. Because of that I ended up having to take the long way over to Layla's old house.

By then I'd convinced myself that she'd decided to make a run for it. Maybe she got to the house, had a moment of clarity and decided to leave me. Maybe she saw the roads, and took the first one out of town. In any case, I didn't see a future worth living without her. I thought about it, but none would have been much more than my own living hell. I'd been without her for only a few hours at that point, and look how quickly everything went to shit.

When I got to the house, none of the lights were on, but someone had definitely been inside. The blinds were open, and Darius had left one of his toys out on the front of the lawn. At that point, it was clear to me that she didn't run. Something went wrong.

Hearing the sirens flare up in the background, I thought that it might be best to warn Buzzy. As I walked into the house, I called him and warned him that some people may be coming for him. If they were looking for me, the chances were that he'd be going down too. It didn't seem right to involve anyone else into the chaos that my life had become. I told him to just comply. When I was done there, his apartment was next on my list. For better or for worse… I had nowhere else to go.

When I got into the house, it looked like a war zone. There was furniture and broken glass spread out all over the floors. The dishes had been thrown from the cabinets and there was a knife with blood on it in the center of the floor. I pulled out my gun and searched every room.

Needless to say I freaked the fuck out. I think that I woke up a few neighbors; at least that's what I could tell from the amount of lights that had flickered on. I closed the shades and tried calling Layla a few more times. Those few more times, it again went straight to voicemail. My head was pounding, my hands were shaking and I couldn't push down the thoughts of my worst fears coming true as I usually did. I was lost.

I went into the kitchen, got some of the brandy that Layla and I had drank on our first night together, sat on the couch—with the intention of drinking myself into oblivion—and waited; for something… for anything.

As I sat there holding back tears, I heard a car pull up right behind mine. Any normal day, I probably would've made my way to the window, or maybe even out the front door with my gun blazin'. But I didn't care. The only person that I wanted to speak to was the one responsible for that shit.

I heard the car door close and soon after someone started fidgeting with the knob. I raised my gun to the door. I put the safety on, just in case I'd made a huge mistake and Layla had come looking for me as well. When the door flew open, I pulled the trigger—just so that the intruder would hear the click and be shaken.

"What the fuck, Anthony!"

"Grant? What the fuck to yourself! I don't have time for your bullshit right now."

"Listen, we need to talk. Can I come in?"

"And how do I know you won't pull anything?"

"You don't. But if it makes you feel any better, I've been suspended. I couldn't arrest you if I wanted to."

"Suspended for what?"

"Apparently my bosses don't look too kindly on letting an informant get their hand cut off."

"You fuckin' think!?"

"Listen. I was out of bounds. I get that and I'm sorry. Now would you please put the fucking gun down and let me in. We don't have much time."

I didn't believe him, but I let him in anyway. I figured—worst-case scenario—I wouldn't feel too bad about killing this motherfucker. I wanted to kill something. He came in the room and sat down beside me.

He looked like he'd just been to fucking war, and smelled like it too. His body was bandaged almost as fully as mine was. He clearly hadn't shaved and, from the smell and look of him, he'd been up for some time, drinking away what had to have been a rough dismissal for him. Good for him though. After all the shit that he put us through, it was nice to see him hit a breaking point. Had this been any other situation I probably would've killed him.

"It's good to see you. I'm glad that you're okay."

"Why the fuck wouldn't I be?"

"Do you not know what's going on?"

"That I'm speaking to the man that tried to send me to jail forever. Yea… I'm quite aware of that."

"Look. I'm not apologizing twice."

Grant turned on the television. Layla had gotten into the habit of watching the news whenever I wasn't around, so he didn't have to turn the channel. It was in the middle of a report that I would've seen, had I just let her keep her bad habit.

"Officers are nearly done with their roundup of all those deemed responsible for the terrorist attack on a local church. We have reports that, after the torrid end to a massive firefight with the terrorists, the officer who had been leading that investigation has been suspended due to what many are calling incompetence. Reporters are told that a new case has been opened with the specific goal of finding and arresting those responsible. We have word that, currently, New City officials are hoping to question a man by the name of Anthony "Black" Boykins. If you have any information on his whereabouts, you are urged to call us at…"

"I know the man covering your case. He's a real hardass, and not one for negotiation. You're gonna need my help."

"What can you do if you're suspended?"

"That's not what I'm talking about."

"What?"

"Have you spoken to Buzzy?"

"Briefly. Maybe about twenty minutes ago. Why?"

"You may want to give him another call."

"Why am I trusting you again?"

"Because right now, you fucking have to."

There's a certain level of sincerity that a person simply can't fake. As much as I hated Grant in that moment, I didn't have anything else to go on, and no clue where Layla and Darius were.

I looked him in the eyes for a few moments. I had a hard time shaking the thoughts of it all being a trap, or another convoluted mishap that he'd concocted just to get me to spill some shit. I even thought about pulling out my gun and ending him where he sat.

Then the reality hit me, as I looked out the window and onto the street. Without him, I was alone and in the dark. Any answers that he could give me were worth me playing along for a few minutes.

I took a pain pill and offered one to Grant—he took one as well. I pulled out my phone and called Buzzy back.

Ring, Ring, Ring

"Buzzy… Buzzy are you there?"

"This ain't Buzzy motherfucker."

"So, I guess it makes no sense to ask then. How are you Vic?"

"What the fuck do you mean: how am I!? Do I even have to say it? Do I even have to fucking say it! I've been locked the fuck up in a cell for months. Smelling other niggas piss and shit, all because of you motherfuckers! I get out, and I find out that you're with my girl!"

"Listen. Vic… it wasn't—"

"Shut the fuck up! I was not fucking finished!"

I heard Layla crying in the background. Everything in my heart and soul shut down when she screamed for me and I couldn't do anything about it. Vic forced me to listen as he smacked her around Buzzy's apartment. I had rage. The kind of rage that you only get when you know that someone's going to have to die for things to be okay.

"You better still be there, motherfucker!"

"I'm here."

"Now, I really don't give a flying fuck about this ho, or that fucking junkie. What I want is my money. I want *all* of it!"

"And how exactly do you want me to do that? Haven't you seen the news? I'm a wanted man. Even if I had it, any time I spend on the road is a risk. Why don't you just come back here?"

"If you try to tell me what to do one more goddamn time, I swear to fucking Christ that I will murder this bitch slow while you listen. You've got four hours to figure that shit out. No calls. No games. No bullshit. Four hours, half a million… you hear me?"

"I got you."

"No fucking funny business, Black. If I get even the slightest thought that you're trying to fuck me over, I will start with this ho and keep cutting off body parts until there's nothing left."

"Understood."

"Four hours, Black!"

He hung the phone up before I could ask him anything. Even if I wanted to, there's really no negotiation with a man when he's in that state. There was no mind-fuck to take advantage of. No leverage. I needed to find the money, or I was fucked.

I started to tear the apartment apart again. I had already been through it a few times, but I was hoping that I may have missed something. Maybe, Layla managed to stash it somewhere that I wouldn't look. As I searched around manically—Grant just watched me from the couch. His face was filled with guilt and regret.

"Are you gonna fucking help me or what?"

"I'm just waiting for you to calm down Anthony."

"Calm down! What the fuck do you mean calm down? Do you know what this motherfucker just said? I've got four fucking hours, Grant. So either help me, or get the fuck out of my way."

"The money's not here Anthony."

"What the fuck are you talking about?"

I stopped my search all at once. I was more surprised that he'd even known what I was talking about. I went over to him, as he threw his head down in shame and placed a blinking chip on the coffee table.

"When you went missing the second time, I made a point to have this place bugged. I figured that, if you were to have gone anywhere, at some point you'd end up back here."

I grabbed the blinking chip and broke it between my fingers. "What the fuck?"

"How do you think that I knew you were here Anthony?"

I gave him a right-hook to his jaw. As unproductive as it was, after all this shit that he'd brought into my life, he had it coming anyway.

“Tell me everything you know.” I put my gun to his head. “Or I swear to God that I will kill you where you sit!”

“Calm the fuck down would ya?”

He was right. I wasn’t thinking clearly. I was just reacting. I wasn’t used to acting out of emotion anymore. Had it been anyone else, I probably would’ve killed them. The only thing that stopped me from taking out Grant for good was the fact that he had the information and connections that I would need if I wanted to get this done the smart way. I put the gun down and listened to what he had to tell me.

“I figured that you would come back here at one point or another, so I had the place bugged. Just in case you didn’t come back, I wanted to make sure to keep tabs on Layla and Darius as well. When they went missing alongside of you, I had to resort to some less traditional methods.”

“Like what Grant?”

“I got in a bit too deep. I just wanted to be the best Anthony, I hope that you know that. I would never intentionally hurt anyone, especially not a mother or child.”

“What the fuck did you do Grant?”

“I did some evidence tampering with Victor Price’s file. I had just gotten the clearance, so I didn’t expect anyone to really notice. The man is a repeat offender—he shouldn’t have been allowed out so easily, at least not with restrictions.”

“So…”

“It’s my fault that he’s out. His entire case has been dismissed. My bosses are furious and I’m probably out of a job.”

“You’re lucky that I don’t fucking kill you.”

“I understand if you do, but I’m here to help. But right now, with the streets literally littered with people trying to see you behind bars or in a body bag, I’m the best friend you’ve got. New City police look out for one another. I can get you around undetected.”

It took everything I had in me not to strangle that man to death and watch him drown on his own vomit. But he was right… I needed him.

“Undetected isn’t the main issue. I need the money.”

“That’s just the thing Anthony. He has the money.”

“What?”

“Like I said. We’ve been doing surveillance on the house. I saw the whole thing go down.”

In the House

(Buzzy)

“Are you alright Lay?”

“I’m fine Buzzy. Where’s Darius?”

After Vic had gotten off the phone with Black, he busted Layla over the head two or three times with the butt of his gun. He was definitely coked out of his mind and not thinking straight. Any normal person would have been able to tell that Layla had been starting to get a bit of a belly. I guess it’s better that he didn’t. If he did, he might have given her those few hits to her stomach instead of her head.

When she came to, he had gone to the bathroom. He took Darius with him as insurance that, while he was in there—probably taking a shit—Layla and I wouldn’t get any bright ideas about running or calling the cops. I helped her back up and laid her on the couch. Once her eyes stopped rolling around her head, I asked her what happened.

“Black and I had planned to meet back at the hotel. I assumed that he was going to call you.”

“He did. He told me not to worry about much, and that he was still alive. Then a few minutes later you and that psychopath were in here playing ‘let’s scare the fuck out of Buzzy’.”

"Do you really think that this is funny right now?"

"No. I know it's not. I just make jokes when I'm nervous."

"Well, man the fuck up would you?"

"I never thought I'd thank someone for hitting a woman in the head, but I'm getting close."

"Buzzy!"

"I'm sorry. So what happened?"

Not long after they got to Layla's house to get the money, Vic popped up with a shotgun, a revolver, and a nose full of *white*—with a look in his eyes like he thought he was Tony fucking Montana.

I wasn't sure if Black knew that he was getting out soon or whatever, but apparently his plan was to get all of the money and get the fuck out of dodge before the police ended up catching up with his ass. Obviously, Vic had a similar idea and all of a sudden here the fuck we are.

"So, if he's got the money, what the fuck is trying to get from Black?"

"I don't know. I mean, he's got everything that he knows about us having. The only other thing that I can think of is 'plan-zero', or whatever the hell that Tony was talking about."

"Oh shit!"

I tried to tell Black while I was locked up that, in my first week, I may have slipped and told a few people about the money in the safe house. I wasn't sure if it was still there, but I had been kicking the shit really bad in jail. At that time I thought that the motherfucker had forgotten about me, and traded the information for a few shots of 'get well'.

I'm not sure how Vic might have found out about that, but the house wasn't even ours anymore. It was Carlos's, and who knows if that motherfucker was even alive anymore?

"Buzzy... Buzzy why do you look like you did something?"

"Nothing. I'm just thinking that we might be in for a long night."

I didn't want to tell her. Not that I saw the point in lying at the time; not even because I was afraid to tell Black. More than likely, whatever I knew, he knew too—or was about to find out quicker than I could reach him to tell him. Besides, Layla didn't need any more stress in her fuckin' life.

And... okay... *Fuck you*—I may have been shitting a few bricks too. But, who wouldn't! That coked-out giant was gettin' ready to blow our fuckin' heads off man. So, yea. I told a white lie. Sue me.

"Do you think we should try to fight?"

"And risk that motherfucker killing one of us? That's probably not the best idea."

"Then what are we supposed to do? Just sit here and wait?"

"Listen. Whatever it is that we do will only make shit worse, especially as long as we're locked up in this fuckin' apartment. Our best bet is to wait."

"And if Tony can't get the money?"

"Listen. I know that you two are in love and all of that other shit. But you don't know Black like I know Black. He'll find a way to get the money, and if he can't he'll find a way to get us out of here. Simple as that. We just have to play it smart in the meantime."

"I don't know Buzzy. I'm worried about him. He was hurt really bad when I was with him earlier. He needs time to rest."

"That man is basically unbreakable. Don't stress it."

We heard the toilet flush and Darius ran into the room to comfort his mother. Vic's heavy ass footsteps followed shortly after. I took the free second to tell Layla not to worry.

"That motherfucker Black is too smart to lose."

I'm not sure if it helped, but I at least had to try to convince my damn self. Every minute seemed to pass by too fast.

As Darius bragged to her about his father letting him get his bag with all of his toys in it back, she got this *crazy* look her eyes. When he handed it her, she opened it and started searching like a mad woman. When she found what she was looking for, she flashed the inside of the bag to me.

I whispered to her. "Who the fuck gives a gun to a kid?"

"Your friend. And relax. It's not loaded. But Vic doesn't know that."

"You willing to risk our lives over a bluff? You crazy as cat-shit!"

"Would you settle the fuck down? It's just an idea."

"For what?"

"Just in case."

She buried the gun under the toys and gave it back to Darius. Vic came into the room—his eyes were red as a fuckin' Bulls jersey. He pulled some coke from out of his pocket and set up some tracks on the table.

"Buzzy, you getting down on this?"

I picked a bad fuckin' time to get clean.

Partners

"So he already has the money?"

"I'm afraid so, Anthony."

It didn't make any sense. Either Vic was out of his fucking mind, or he just wanted to squeeze every penny that he could out of me while he had the upper hand. Neither made a difference in what I had to do at the moment. Though it may've been a better idea to think of his motivations before I reacted. It's hard to keep your thoughts straight in those kinds of situations.

"So, do you have a plan?"

"I'm working on one, but you're not gonna like it."

"Well, anything short of breaking into the police department, and I don't see why not."

"That all depends on where Carlos is right now."

Assuming that Carlos was still alive, he would be my only way back into my old safe house. The only money that I had left to my name was either in Vic's possession, or lining the walls of that lunatic's new home.

I did everything that I could to think of another way to get the money for Vic, while Grant made a few phone calls to the people in the department that he hoped still had his back. I didn't really care to hear the lies and promises that he had to make to get them back on his side.

While he was on the phone, I toyed with a few other ways to go about the situation without having to threaten my freedom. I could've tried to trick Vic with some fake cash or a mix of that and whatever cash I could get. It would be in a duffel bag or some shit like that.

Assuming that he was already thinking like the kingpin he pretended to be, there was no way that he wouldn't check it. Even if he didn't, the bigger issue was that he had all three of them. Something like that would be risky enough with one person. With three people, it'd be damn near impossible for all of us to get out of there; especially when—going by the tone of his voice—he intended to kill me as soon as he got the money.

But the one thing that he wouldn't be expecting was Grant. I wasn't sure how much I could trust him to stick to his word and stay loyal as all of this shit went down but, like he said, he was the only friend that I had. It was either accept his help, or let him fumble himself into another fuck up that could leave my family dead.

"Alright. Carlos is actually on his way downtown. He just left the ICU and will be going to the holding to await his transition. Will a phone call work for you?"

"No. Niggas like that won't do phone calls. Can you have your boys bring him here, or can we meet them somewhere?"

"Absolutely not. I've got three, maybe four people that will help me out max. It isn't on the best of terms and none of them are assigned to his transport."

"When's the next time that one of your guys will be near him?"

"Probably when he gets to holding. But, at that point, he'll be on the books. I'm suspended, Anthony. They won't let me anywhere near him."

"Who said you?"

All I would need is five minutes for Carlos to make the call. It would be risky but, if he gave the order to his goons, they would have to leave me alone and let me get the cash without interference or intimidation.

I had close to a million in those walls. That would be enough to pay off Vic—and after we finished that whole debacle Layla and I could get a decently-sized house upstate. We'd still have to work, but fuck it. I thought that we could just cross that bridge when we got there. Besides, a couple hundred grand isn't a bad start by any means.

"Please don't tell me that you're saying what I think you're saying."

"I'm not saying it, I'm just getting up. Now, if you excuse me, I've got to figure out a way to get in and out of prison in less than an hour."

"How the fuck are you gonna do that?"

“That my friend, depends on how strictly you keep your word.”

“So we’re breaking into a prison?”

“Not exactly.”

I took a few more shots of whiskey, and walked past Grant to the car.

“I’ll tell you the plan on the way. We don’t have a lot of time.”

The truth was I didn’t have a plan at all. I knew that it’d be a longshot, but the only thing that I could think to do was get to the cell and get to Carlos. I’d hoped that he’d be able to give me something that I could use.

Honestly, it was a half-cocked idea if it was anything at all. But I had to try.

Monsters

We had three hours left by the time that we got down to the station. The plan was complicated, but straightforward enough to explain to Grant on the drive there.

He knew the main guy in booking and, as a bonus, the late nightshift happened to be a disgruntled lazy bunch. Because of that, they would often turn the cameras off so that they could doze off or do whatever nefarious thing that cops were up to when no one's watching.

Grant would call his guy and set up a blank drop. They would sign me in under an alias with the charge of public intoxication. It wasn't a big enough charge to garner much attention. As a matter of fact, in New City, it's pretty common. I'd be expedited to the drunk tank—if they bothered to do the paperwork—and I would wait there while Carlos completed his intake.

Once Carlos was dropped off and the arresting officers debriefed and sent away, Grant's guy would escort him to—you guessed it—the drunk tank. I would have a long enough time with Carlos to get him to call down his dogs, in exchange for a cut of the money and a few painkillers to hold him over until he got to the *big house*.

It seemed easy enough, but my biggest worry was whether or not I could trust Grant. Just a day prior to that, he would've served my head up on a fucking pike just to get one of those bullshit little trophies for him to pin on his pelt. Now, he seemed like he wanted—more than anything—to help me. I wasn't buying the "guilty conscience" bullshit but worst-case scenario, if he happened to have a sudden change of heart, I had a contingency plan.

"Are you sure that this is the only way? Once you're in there, I won't be able to get you out until the time's up. If you miss him by even a moment, or if there's any kind of slip-up… you're done for."

"I understand that. And as long as you're not the reason that the shit goes south, we won't have any problems."

"What the fuck does that mean?"

"It means that we're allies of circumstance. You'd do well not to forget that, because I haven't."

"Hey, in case you forgot, I'm the one helping you. So you can cut that 'lone wolf', tough-guy shit out right now!"

"And why the fuck are you helping me exactly Grant? So you can get another fucking pin?"

"No, that's not the fucking reason Anthony."

"What do you like me or some shit? You into dudes! Motherfucker keep your eyes on the road… I don't do that shit."

"Anthony, are you fucking drunk?!"

I was a little drunk. Unintentionally, I assure you. I'd convinced myself that it was necessary to get into character.

"Holy shit! What the fuck is wrong with you? Do you realize that if literally *anything* goes wrong, they'll put me in a cell right next to you?"

"Easy. Easy. I was just fucking around... Jesus."

"Don't you fuck this up!"

"Seriously, Grant. Why the fuck are you helping me?"

"Because I don't want to see you lose another family Anthony."

"What...?"

It was true. Almost seven years ago to the day, my son was killed by stray fire from a rival gang. It was my fault. I was young and stupid—too proud to know when it was time to call it quits.

As it turns out, there was another young and dumb motherfucker out there that day. I mentioned before that it was the first time in my life that I had ever called the police. Grant had still been a beat cop back then. He was one of the first officers to respond to the scene.

Apparently, the reason he was so insistent on using my first name is because, for weeks prior to that—when they had planned to arrest me—he was also tapped to be a part of the squadron to come take me in, or take me to jail. At that time, they didn't really care which—I was enough of a public nuisance that they just wanted me off of the streets.

"After that day, I knew that you were broken. Hell, who wouldn't be? We tossed your case and deemed you as inactive. We'd assumed that you'd gone into hiding or were working somewhere behind the scenes. You were no longer a threat, so we left you alone. The evidence was flimsy anyway."

"And you just tell me now?"

"Fuck… I thought you knew. Why do you think I kept letting you go see your girl?"

"Then why try to kill me?"

"You brought that on your damn self. I was trying to offer you a way out before all of this shit went sideways."

"Why?"

"Because, I could've very easily been you. A few bad choices. The wrong neighborhood. The wrong girl. I know that you just did what you had to do to survive, so I sympathize. Poor me for being human, right?"

I really didn't know what to say. It was a mind fuck, but it certainly helped me sober up before the drop.

"What are you gonna tell me next…? That Buzzy's your godson?"

"No. I just hate that asshole."

I did my best not to laugh. It was inappropriate, but fuck it—everything had been going wrong; my head was pounding, I was fucked up, and voluntarily going to jail to interrogate a motherfucker who cut my best friend's hand off so that I could get the money to pay off my baby-momma's baby-daddy.

If I was ever going to laugh—even out of pure fear and anxiety—that was the last time that I'd get a chance to do it for a while. Grant laughed right along with me. We got to the station a few minutes after our "heart-to-heart".

***

"I'm gonna have to put you in cuffs. Just make sure that you keep your head down, and try not to attract too much attention on your way in."

Grant put my arms behind my back and cuffed them there. I didn't have much to say as he walked me to the back door of the police station. I'd like to think that he knew enough not to cross me. Besides, threats would have just been distracting.

He pulled my hood over my head, to make me seem more down and out than I really was. I didn't think that it'd be too necessary to "pretend" that I was at my wits end; the liquor had still been hitting me pretty badly, and my concussion caused my vision to go in and out pretty frequently, so I wasn't worried about looking the part.

We waited at the back door for his friend on the inside to meet us. When he came, Grant informed him that we had an hour. I didn't trust the code speak, but it was too late for second thoughts and opinions on speech. I was in the station and Grant watched as the door closed behind me.

His friend took us through the same catacombs that they'd interrogated Buzzy and I in almost a month earlier. It's amazing how different shackles and cells can look when you have no intention of staying there. We went past the sealed off rooms and up the stairs to the main halls.

Grant's man took special care not to put me around anyone that may squeal on him for what he was doing. My presence notwithstanding, the door from which he came in was only supposed to be used on certain orders. He quipped that, if they didn't have enough bad people, the officers would just use it for their extramarital affairs and various forms of fucking over inmates. That's not the kind of thing you say to a guy like me; but, lucky for him, I was in no position to correct him.

When we finally got to the drunk-tank it was empty and the lights were dimmed.

"There you go, we got it all set-up for you. Just remember; from the second that he gets here, you've got five minutes."

"Got it."

He left me alone in the cell. Fortunately—due to the circumstances—there were no pat-downs. I still had my gun and my blade. Even if Carlos wanted to put up a fight, I had what I needed to make quick work of any non-compliance he had. I promised Grant that I wouldn't kill the guy—and by that, I meant that I would do my best not to.

***

By minute fifteen, there was still no sign of Carlos, nor anyone else for that matter. I started to panic. What if Grant had finally gotten me? What if this had all just been some fucking trap? A long fucking trap?! It may have been the liquor that I'd drank earlier but I started to freak the fuck out. Just as I started plotting my escape, I heard from the main door.

"Down inmate!"

Three officers walked into the room alongside Grant's guy. They looked me up and down, and asked me my name.

"Rodger."

"What the fuck kind of name is Rodger?"

Apparently it was show-time—"Rodger Dodger baby. Killin' it from here to wonderland—sacrificing for the greater good!"

One of the officers screamed to Grant's guy, "Hey Larry! What the fuck is this?"

"It's the drunk-tank. What the fuck do you expect? Just leave that asshole in there while we get his paperwork done. That guy's harmless."

Larry. I'd have to remember that name, though I'm pretty sure that he and Grant had kept it on the hush-hush for a reason; it's always smart to have your contacts in line.

"Alright. But if they start scrapping, I'm holding you accountable."

They opened my cell door and pushed Carlos in to sit right beside me. He recognized me as soon as they closed his cell door. He was wise enough to keep his fucking mouth shut until they left.

***

He stared at me for a minute before he said anything. It was odd, but I just put it off on whatever the fuck they'd been pumping into him at the hospital. When he finally collected his thoughts, he smiled. A bunch of his teeth had been knocked out, his eyes were glassed over and he definitely shouldn't have been discharged from the hospital.

Despite his appearance, he seemed to be thinking clearly enough. Besides, I was never one for over-caring about a motherfucker's physical state. If his heart was beating, he was alive enough for me. He cut me off before I could speak.

“Are you here to kill me Negro? If so, I'm afraid that there's a line.”

He looked more sane than I was used to seeing him. I guess the bit of time in the hospital and away from *the life* helped him to gain some perspective on reality. It bothered me that he didn't have his usual half-cocky, half-omniscient tone; but it wasn't the time for delving into his spiritual growth either. As hard as it was, I had to focus.

“I'm not here to kill you. I need to ask you for a favor.”

“Tisk, tisk, Negro. Does it really look like I'm in a position to grant favors? We're behind bars.”

I reached into my pocket and grabbed my cellphone.

"But we're not limited."

"How the hell did you get that in here?"

"It's a long story. Listen, I don't have much time."

He looked at me as if he'd just realized what had been going on and began to laugh so hard that snot came out of his nose. It was unsettling. When motherfuckas played those kinds of games with me in the past, I would start breaking bones, but it was clear that my former tactics wouldn't work. That nigga was already dead in his mind. I had to find a way to break through his wall of lunacy. I thought to myself: *stay basic, keep it simple*.

"What the hell is wrong with you?"

He wiped his nose, and then the tears from his eyes.

"I told him. I told him and he didn't believe me. You truly are a fighter! Aren't you Negro? Such persistence. You and I could've made a lot of money together."

"Carlos! I need you to focus."

"Okay, Negro. Okay. What can I do for you?"

"I need you to call your guys and tell them that I need to get something from the safe house."

"And what's that?"

"I'd rather not say."

"It wouldn't be the money in the bedroom walls would it?"

Everything in my mind fell apart. I didn't know what to say. I just stared at him until my hands shook and my head dropped.

"Yes, Negro. It's gone. It's all gone. You thought that I wouldn't gut the house before making it my home. Come on Negro! You're better than that!"

I pulled the gun from my hip and put it to his head. "Where is it?"

He didn't give a fuck about death. He just pressed his forehead against the barrel and kept on laughing at me.

"Go ahead Negro. Please. There's nothing but death for any of us at the end of the day."

It was useless to threaten him. Even if I did kill him, the sound alone would alert the officers outside. No matter what deal I'd made with Grant, all that shit would've been out the window if his boys returned to see me in the cell with a gun—and another suspect on the ground with a bullet in his brain.

"Easy Negro. It's okay. Death will come for you soon as well."

"It already has. But you've just killed my family."

"Victor... I guess he *wasn't* full of shit."

"What do you mean?"

“As a professional courtesy Negro, I will share something with you… For a price, of course.”

I looked at the time. We only had a minute or two left, before the guard would come back to let me free. At that point this entire trip had seemed like a waste of fucking time. My family would be dead, and I’d be hunted. Defeated, I just gave Carlos the pill bottle of painkillers and told him to “Go ahead.”

He pounced on the bottle like a vulture, and took enough of it to kill a man who hadn’t built up such a hefty tolerance. He spoke to me as he crushed some up of it into powder to snort.

“You were never supposed to live this long Negro. Not you; not Buzzy. Even Lenny wasn’t meant to die how he did. That way was sloppy.”

He snorted a bump of the dust off of the bench and continued.

“Nope. Nope. All three of you were supposed to die later on that night.”

“What night?”

“What night do you think Negro…? The pharmacy.”

“That was months ago. What the fuck are you talking about?”

Vic and Carlos had been working together since the pharmacy job a few months back. Before we met at the rendezvous point, he had actually just come from a business meeting with the cholos.

Carlos told me that the idea had been in the works for some time, but Vic and Lenny didn't have the technical skills to get the job done. Buzzy and I were known for our intricate jobs. They figured that they could use us to get in and out without having to worry about being detected.

When Buzzy had been getting high with Vic and Lenny a few weeks before that, they offered him a spot on the team under the condition that I would be a part of the whole thing with them. Buzzy volunteered us, and a few months later here the fuck we all were. Worse for wear, and most of us dead or dying.

"We were supposed to meet at the safe house with Victor and Lenny after he put a bullet in the back of your head. You were never supposed to make it out alive, cabron."

"If that's true, then why didn't you just kill me when you had the chance to?"

"You know why Negro. I'm a businessman before anything. When you have the opportunity to use your competition to make money, you take it. The better man won that day. I adjusted accordingly."

"What else do you know?"

"I know everything, cabron. We've never stopped watching the things that you do. You're one of the few men that can strike fear into the hearts of others. It's a good quality. It can make some men seem like gods. You know—better than I—how beneficial that can be."

"I asked you... What else do you know?"

"I know that he wants us dead. And I know that he will get his wish."

As Carlos snorted another bump of the pill off of the bench, Larry came back with his keys in hand. "Time's up!"

He opened the cell door and waited for me on the side.

"I'm serious. If I have to close this door, it won't be opening for a long time."

Carlos waved goodbye to me as I walked out of the cell and Larry put the cuffs back around my wrist.

"I'll see you in hell, Negro!"

As I was walked to the end of the hall and out of the back of the police station, Carlos put the bottle to his lips and ate the remainder of the pills. He was careful enough to hide it in his pocket. He smiled, as he gulped them down.

I'd find out later that he died from the pills. I don't think that he'd done it accidentally. As ferocious as Carlos was on the streets, he'd have a good portion of that power zapped the moment that he walked into a prison.

We make a lot of enemies in the bracket of business. I'm sure that he had finally hit the same point that I had, where he finally just wanted it to all be over. It was a sensible end. They would have killed him at some point in the near future. Sometimes, it's more respectable to just take the initiative upon yourself.

It probably helped that he had basically lost his fucking mind. Not much. But it had to have made it easier.

Hopeless

I suddenly had even more to worry about. With no money and no help from Carlos, I was at a complete loss. I still had a little over an hour left. I wasn't sure what I would do. In times like that—when you don't know—it's helpful to embrace the purgatory. The mind has a way of solving problems more easily when you think you're not paying any attention to them.

Larry pushed me out of the back door. "I better not see you back here. If I do, you won't be leaving," then he slammed it shut.

"Well, I guess that burns that favor."

Grant uncuffed me as he tried to make light of the situation. I could tell that he was hoping that I'd come back with some good news, but I had nothing. I got in the back of the car, and waited for him to finish his cigarette and get into the driver's seat. As I waited, I let my mind go blank, and stared at the raindrops slowly collecting on the window.

We had an hour left. When he got into the car he asked, "So where to now?"

"The church."

I didn't have any other answer. I was done. I had no more magic tricks; no more secret stashes; no more back-up. I would wait for Vic to call me and, when I showed up with nothing, he would make me watch him kill Buzzy, then Layla, and likely Darius. Depending on how merciful he was feeling, he'd probably kill me too. Either that, or make me live with the pain until I killed myself. It seemed like my future had no options.

"The church? Are you sure?"

"Yea."

Grant pulled out of the alley and headed down the sleek roads; back down to the East Side of town.

***

"Alright, you've been quiet back there for the whole drive. Are you going to tell me the plan or what?"

"There is no plan Grant. Just going to make my peace."

"What the fuck are you talking about? He's gonna kill your girl Anthony!"

"I know what he said. I know what the stakes are. There's just nothing left for me to do."

I didn't really expect him to understand. It was pointless to argue with him. In my mind, I had less than an hour left to go and it would all come to the end that my life had been building toward. I was ready to go, having been fighting the truth for my entire life. I was tired of running. There comes a point in a man's life where he has no moves left but to embrace the devil.

I knew my death would be quick and painless. At the very least, I hoped that it would be. Vic likely wouldn't be able to risk going the torture route. Even if it was possible for him to get away with it, it wasn't really his style. When he killed, it was used more effectively as a way to torture whoever was next. All in all, I'd done the best I could at that point.

As I sat in the back of Grant's car, just contemplating what other things I could do, I was content. I wasn't at peace, but I'd known that everything could be done. The last thing left for me to do was to say my grace and wait for the last call that I would ever get.

"You've got to be kidding me. After all of this! After this whole thing, you're just gonna roll over and let him win?"

"It's not about winning or losing anymore Grant. We had the chance to change that destiny and we lost. Now, all that's left to do is own up to it."

"And your family?"

"They're his family. As much as I lie to myself about it, this is all a result of my own fuck up."

I hadn't even noticed that I was slurring my words. My head had been bothering me ever since the shootout. I hated complaining, but my underplaying of the injury didn't do much to curb the pain. I could barely keep a thought straight in my mind. When Grant noticed, he got out of the driver's seat and checked my bandages.

"Jesus Christ! You're bleeding all over the goddamn seat!"

"You shouldn't say that in front of the church."

"Anthony, you need medical attention. No wonder you're talking crazy! You're fucking delirious."

I didn't think so. I just thought that I was going to see the light. I passed out not long after that. I still don't remember exactly how I got into the church.

***

"It seems that you believe that God has forsaken you, Anthony."

When I woke up Grant was gone. I didn't bother to ask Pastor Joy where he was. Even if I did, the Pastor has a penchant for keeping secrets and telling riddles. I didn't have the time for his *Yoda* bullshit.

When I checked my phone, it was still ten minutes to the hour. Apparently the Pastor had to use his *Epi-pen* to wake me up from the near dead. Grant must've told him what had been going on. He seemed to know exactly what was happening without having to get into too much detail.

My phone battery was low. When I tried to rush myself up to put it on a charger, I almost instantly collapsed back onto the pew.

"Easy, young man. You've had a hell of a night. There's no need for you to rush at this exact moment. Breathe. Relax. Allow your mind to clear."

"Why did you wake me up?"

"Well, I wouldn't want you to miss your engagement this evening. It seems like something that you shouldn't miss."

"Then, you already know."

"I know enough to know that you're considering failure a valid option."

"It's the only one. What else am I supposed to do?"

"Ah, and therein is the question. Questions are problems, and every problem has an exact solution. So tell me, what are your other options?"

"Other than to run the hell away, I'm not sure."

"Certainly, you don't mean that."

"Hey, look, I'm open to suggestions."

I reached to the back of my head. My bandages had been replaced by new ones, and the stitches were redone.

"A quick fix. Courtesy of my time in the military. That should hold you over until you can see a doctor. Or perhaps… a nurse."

I got up and joined Pastor Joy in front of the cross. As I walked up to him, I looked around the church. It had still been in shreds from the shootout. Some friendly parishioners had helped to board up some of the broken windows with wood panels, but there was still a ton of glass and other shit on the ground.

"I'm sorry about the church."

"It's fine son. Inconsequential. I'm more concerned about the other broken pieces."

"Oh come on. Don't start that."

"Just hear me out."

"What is this going to be a story about Jesus or Mary?"

"Judas, actually…"

I've got to admit, I was interested. Who the fuck wouldn't be? Judas is an underused character.

"There are several explanations and rationalizations for why Judas betrayed Christ. However, I choose to believe that the most accurate and possibly the most relevant to your particular situation is this one. The money Anthony. He did it for the money."

"What the hell are you talking about?"

"People like to overcomplicate things and pretend that there's always some master plan at work. Those people—in reality—are far and few between. Most act purely out of simplistic motivation and impulse. If you believe that they—back in the ancient times—were mortal, then it behooves you to decipher their motives in that way. So, simply put, he did it for the money."

"And that means what exactly?"

"It means that, quite often, if you follow the money, you'll find the truth behind it. No games, no strategy—just greed. We are flawed at birth with a proclivity for indulgence in that with which we were warned. So simple are we, that we don't foresee our downfall because of it."

My phone rang before I could respond. Pastor Joy would usually leave the room, but he seemed intent on hearing the conversation. Who gave a shit if he heard it though? I had basically put the man's home in the middle of a war. The least that I could do was to let him eavesdrop.

"Hello?"

"Time's up motherfucker. Do you have my money?"

In the split second before I was going to say no, something clicked in my mind. If Carlos did have the money, and it was stashed in the walls, there would be no reason for him to move it. Even if he did, he would have to split it with everyone else just to save face and seem like the beloved leader of the clan.

It was doubtful that anyone else would go ripping the house apart looking for something that they didn't know was there. The money was still in the house. It had to be. Where else would he have put it?

"Yea, I've got your money."

All I could hope for at that point was enough time to grab it and get to wherever the fuck Vic wanted me to meet him.

“Good. Meet me at the ferry terminal in a half-hour. Come alone, or I’m killing the bitch first.”

He hung up on me. I expected as much. By then everyone under the sun had probably gotten word that I had cooperated with the cops. At least everyone on the streets knew. He would wisely assume that I’d been having the call traced.

I had a half hour to get the money and get to the ferry terminal, just to make sure that everyone was kept alive until I could figure something out. I would have to be quick, but it was possible.

“Thank you, Pastor. I think I’ve got a way out of this shit.”

“That’s good, son. Be safe.”

“I will. Sorry for cursing. I know God doesn’t like that.”

“Dear boy, Jesus didn’t speak English any more than you speak Hebrew. Words are just words. It’s your actions that he cares about.”

I’m pretty sure that I should apologize for those too.

Fate

I took a cab back to Layla's. I didn't bother going inside; I just needed the guns from my trunk. I loaded two of them, screwed on the silencer and drove to the safe house. I had twenty minutes to get in, get out, and down to the ferry. I circled around the back of the house and snuck in through the bedroom window. Some people had been lurking around, but I was quiet enough not to attract any attention.

The wall that I'd hidden the money in was covered by a large framed picture of Tony Montana. Those motherfuckers really went all out with their drug-fueled aspirations. I moved the picture and there it was: a giant hole in the wall, covered not so discreetly by a thick cloth towel.

When I pulled the towel down and reached into the wall, I felt it. There were bricks of cash behind the poster—even more than I'd originally left behind. I loaded up as much as I could in a duffel bag and put the towel and frame back on the wall. Just as I'd started to make my way back toward the window, I heard the click of a gun behind me.

"What the fuck are you doing here, cabron?"

"Just... hanging out." I slid my gun to the side of me, where Marcus couldn't see it. Had he got wind that I was armed, the intrusion could be considered an act of war.

"I'll ask you one more time, fucker!"

As he walked toward me, I ducked the barrel of his gun and shot him once in each leg. I caught him as he was falling and shoved a bedsheet in his mouth to cover up the noise. When he started to scream, I bashed him over the head a few times with the butt of the gun, until he stopped moving altogether. It was sloppy, but I didn't have time for conversation or pleasantries.

Once he was knocked out, I peeked into the hall to make sure that no one had heard our quick scuffle. When I saw that it was clear, I closed the door and locked it. I took the frame back off, loaded the rest of the cash, and snuck back out through the window. I checked the time on my phone, finding I had ten minutes to get across town. I ran to the car and pulled off the side of the curb as quickly as I could with the money in the passenger seat.

***

I got to the terminal a little after midnight. The ferry in New City was a major point of transport during the day, but at that time of night there was hardly anybody there. There were two separate parking lots.

The main lot remained open for the employees that worked the overnight; the second was usually closed around eight. The ramp to the lot was usually blocked off by some shitty traffic cones. People would take them as a suggestion and use the lot anyway. It essentially became the place where people did all their nefarious shit in the dark and out in the open at the same time. My phone had died, but I knew that had to be where Vic would want to meet.

As I drove in, it didn't look like anyone was there yet. I took the opportunity to park in the middle. It was a far point away from the exits, but it gave me a clear route out if I ended up having to make a run for it. As a bonus, I was able to see every corner—just in case Vic had decided to bring some company along with him. It was a risk to trust that he would come alone, but I had no other option.

I got out of the car and lit a cigarette. I left the car running, but I turned off the headlights so that I wouldn't be too easily spotted. It wouldn't buy me much time, but I had to be as ready as I could in case the worst went down.

As I checked the clip of my gun to make sure that it was loaded, a car pulled slowly down the ramp. It was hard to make out at first but, as it pulled closer, I could tell that it was Layla's. I grabbed the bag of money from the passenger seat and threw it onto the hood of the car. As the car pulled up a few yards ahead of me, I recognized Layla in the driver's seat. She looked worried, but more together than you'd expect from someone who'd just been taken hostage. I tried to look deeper into the car but, as the rains continued, all I could make out was her oddly static driving posture.

She parked the car and dropped her hands from the wheel. After a few seconds, Buzzy got out of the seat next to her and stood beside the car, looking just as terrified as Layla was. Vic shouted something to him from the backseat and he began walking slowly toward the car.

"Buzzy! Are you alright?"

"I'm good man, just wait until I get there."

He kept darting his eyes back to the car. I still couldn't see Vic, but he had to be there; everyone was acting as if they had bombs strapped to their backs. I waited for Buzzy to approach, assuming that he would just rattle off whatever orders Vic had barked at them on the drive over.

As the rains started up again, Buzzy seemed more willing to try to talk to me. I saw the flicker of a match-light illuminate the back of Layla's car and was able to make out Vic in the backseat, as he lit whatever it was that he was smoking.

"Black! That you man?"

"Of course it's me. Who'd you expect?"

"I'll be honest man, I don't know. This day has been fucked up."

"Who you telling? How are they?"

He twitched a little bit as he answered. It was physical quirk that he only had when he was on some shit.

"They. They, good."

"What about you?"

"Been better."

As Buzzy came closer I was able to make out his swollen jaw and bloodshot eyes.

"What the fuck happened?"

"Hold on Black. I'm supposed to stop here, until I see the light."

Buzzy looked back and waited for Vic to light another cigarette, or whatever the fuck it was that he was smoking. As soon as he saw the wick light up, he proceeded forward.

"I'm supposed to pat you down and check the bag. Just make sure that you don't move. That crazy motherfucker's got a gun to Lay's head."

As he gave me a bullshit pat down—he explained to me what'd been going on.

"He told me to pat you down, and bring the bag back to him."

"And what guarantee do I have that he'll let you guys go?"

"None. We never got that far. He wants me to just bring the bag to him and, after that, I'm pretty sure that he's just gonna pull the fuck off."

"How the fuck is that supposed to work?"

"I don't know. I was hoping that you had a plan."

I didn't. Foolishly, I had sort of just hoped that he would let this run smooth. I had to think quick. If I couldn't get Vic to get out of the car, we'd all be dead.

"I'm sorry, Buzzy."

As he checked me, I elbowed him in the back of the head. While he was on the ground cursing, I threw the bag of money back in the car and pulled out my gun. While Vic tried to figure out what the fuck was going on, Layla dove out of the driver seat and ran toward me screaming.

"Layla, get down!"

Vic jumped out of the backseat, and started letting off bullets. As I ducked to meet Layla behind the car I came in, I did my best to count the shots that he'd let off.

"Are you okay?"

"He's still got Darius!"

"You think he's crazy enough to shoot his own son?"

Before she could respond, Vic reached into the car, grabbed Darius by his collar and dragged him out.

"I'm not fucking with you Black!" he screamed, with one hand around Darius's neck and the other pointing a gun on top of his head. "Give me the fucking money!"

He may've had two or three shots left to let off. I gave Layla a gun.

"If anything goes wrong, you shoot this motherfucker!"

She didn't answer me. I can't blame her too much for being shaken up, but I didn't have time to console her.

"Let him go, and I'll give you the money!"

“You think this is a fucking game?”

Vic put the gun to the back of Darius and shot him through the left shoulder. Layla’s screams, along with the gunshot, had to have attracted some attention. I was suddenly on new time constraints. I got up and checked to make sure that Darius was still alive. He was crying and rolling around on the ground—but he was okay. I dropped my gun and grabbed the bag.

“Just take the fucking money, and get the hell out of here.”

Vic was clearly high out of his mind. He kept darting his head around; paranoid that the cops would be coming. He pointed the gun back at Darius and put his other hand out to grab the bag from me.

As I walked toward him, he let off the rest of his clip. One of the shots missed; the other hit me in the stomach. I didn’t care how bad the damage was, I just wanted it to be over. I walked for as far as I could before my legs gave out. I did my best to stay up on my knees and dropped the bag in front of me. As I gripped my stomach and keeled over, I watched as his footsteps came closer to me and listened as he reloaded his gun.

“I’ve got to hand it to you Black. You had me worried for a minute there that this shit wouldn’t work out.”

He kicked me in my stomach as he locked in the clip.

“After everything that we’ve been through together, imagine my fucking surprise when I come out of jail—for a crime that *you* started—just to find out that you took my kindness, and started fucking my girl." He pulled the hammer back on the gun and continued to scream at me. "Get up motherfucker! Get the fuck up! I want you to look me dead in my fucking eyes and beg me not to kill you!"

"I ain't beggin' you for shit."

He lifted my head up and swung clean at my jaw. When I fell to the ground, it was into a puddle of my own blood. He lifted me up again by my neck.

"Beg motherfucker!" He put the gun under my chin. "I said 'beg!'"

When I tried to speak my mouth was filled with blood. As it dripped from my teeth, I smiled at him, then turned my head to Layla and told her that I loved her. When I turned my head back to Vic, I closed my eyes as he pulled the trigger.

The gun jammed.

When Buzzy noticed, he stood and dove to tackle Vic to the ground. Layla ran from the side of the car while the two scuffled in the rain and pointed her gun at Vic's head. When he froze, Buzzy stood up and kicked him in the head like he played for the fuckin' NFL. It didn't knock him out, but he was stunned bad enough that he was no longer an immediate issue.

Layla rushed to Darius and checked his wound and blood pressure. Buzzy helped me up and took me to the car.

"What the fuck man? Have you lost your damn mind?"

"I had to get him out of the car Buzz."

"Well you did that, and you hit me in my fuckin' stomach. Now I gotta get you back."

He laid me on the seat, as I tried to force out a laugh.

"You gonna be okay man. Hey Layla, come on. We gotta get the fuck up outta here."

Layla picked up Darius and got in the backseat with me. As Buzzy got ready to drive us away, a car with sirens pulled into the parking lot and stopped in front of Vic's semi-paralyzed body on the ground.

***

As the police car approached, Buzzy got out and laid face-down on the cement with his hands up. The car stopped right next to Vic and the driver got out. I couldn't see who it was, but it didn't seem like they were too surprised by the scene. He walked up to the car door where I was and opened it.

"Jesus Christ, Anthony!"

Grant looked in the car and saw that the three of us were still alive. As soon as he saw that we were safe, he told Buzzy to get the hell off of the ground and handcuffed Vic. When he walked back over to us, he seemed concerned, but not necessarily about the blood or the gunshot wounds.

"You all need to get the fuck out of here. Now!"

"How the fuck did you find us?"

Grant reached into my pocket and broke open my phone to reveal that he'd put a tracker in it.

"Now get the hell out of here. They're going to be looking for you."

"Who?"

"Everyone. Now go. I'll be in touch when I can."

Buzzy got back into the driver's seat and put the car in drive. Before he pulled off, Grant urged him: "Whatever the fuck you do, stay off of the main roads."

He tapped the top of the car twice and put Vic in his backseat. As Buzzy drove out of the lot and down the back road, Layla did what she could to stop Darius's bleeding. The three of them were frantic, but it seemed like they were going to be okay.

As Buzzy picked up speed, Grant followed behind us and kept pace as long as he could. As a fleet of police cars passed us and drove into the lot, Buzzy started to pray.

Layla called to me and told me to stay awake. I didn't want to let her know exactly how bad my wound was. I kept applying pressure to the bullet hole, to keep myself from falling asleep. We swerved around a puddle and made a sharp turn down the dirt road. As Grant tried to keep pace, he lost control of his car and it tumbled over in circles, eventually spinning into a guardrail.

As my heart slowed its beating, I tried to force out a whisper to tell Layla that everything would be okay. I don't think that she would've heard me anyway. There was too much going on to pay much focus to one thing.

As I drifted into the darkness, I looked into the rearview mirror. All of the cop cars had been diverted to Grant's wreck beside the guardrail. As they attempted to stop the car from falling into the river, the rains increased and it slowly tipped over and fell off of the side. The sirens blared as officers began jumping in after it.

When I couldn't keep my eyes open any longer, I began to think of all the times that I thought I'd died before. I thought of everything that I'd done to protect my family; I prayed that Buzzy would take care of my unborn child, and asked for forgiveness.

The last thing that I heard before my spirit left me, was the sound of our own car swerving along with the approaching sounds of ambulances and rescue teams. I thought that it might be a good death. I reached my hand out to Layla as she noticed me falling asleep.

"Tony!"

"Tony!"

"Tony!..."

It was the best that I could do back then.

***

Tonight on Eye-Witness News: Officers scramble to rescue four passengers from the Hudson River, after it was flung into the waters below. In an even more bizarre twist, the vehicle is believed to have been harboring Anthony "Black" Boykins. For those of you just joining us, New City Police have been searching for Mr. Boykins for several days. After a close encounter at a hotel where Mr. Boykins is believed to have been hiding out, officials are both tense and mystified by the method of which they were finally able to catch up to him. For more on this story, please stick with us as it unfolds. For Eye-Witness News, I'm Karen Patinkin.

***

Some sins like to make sure that you die a slow death.

Turn the page to get your preview to Trapped in the Game 4!

Black's in trouble again. After surviving the crash off of the New City terminal ramp, and being resuscitated—Black awakens to a whole new list of troubles. With Layla and Buzzy both M.I.A., Black must figure out a way to get of the hospital bed before his survival is discovered by an emboldened Vic—who continues to wreak havoc on New City—in pursuit of his ultimate goal—complete power.

While Black devises a plan, an unknown threat arises in the form of two Detectives—former colleagues of Grant— who will stop at nothing to get to the bottom of Grant's murder and believe Black to be the killer.

With only his wits, his will, and his determination to reunite with the ones he loves—can Black cheat death another day?

In this latest installment watch as New City's greatest criminal faces off with it's greatest threat, and New City's finest. Will this be the end, or can love survive hell?

Turn the page to get your FREE prequel to the Trapped in the Game series!

Get your FREE prequel to the series, Trapped in the Game!

Black and Buzzy very early on in their hustling days. Though they have clearly spent some time in the game -they're not quite the Black and Buzzy that have grown accustomed to. Black is not yet going by his hood-moniker and is instead referred to by his original nickname, Tony.
Tony and Buzzy - having recently sunken in all of their money into drugs- are struggling to make ends meet and contemplating various ways to do so. When Buzzy tells Tony about one of their middle men who've cheated them out of money, they raid his house. An accidental killing leads the two down a tough dark path within…New City.

Made in the USA
Las Vegas, NV
15 February 2021